NIGHT OF THE RED DEVIL

Books by the same author

Haunted House Blues
Meet Me by the Steelmen

For older readers

The Flither Pickers
Riding the Waves

NIGHT OF THE RED DEVIL

THERESA TOMLINSON

Illustrations by

ANTHONY LEWIS

WALKER BOOKS
AND SUBSIDIARIES
LONDON • BOSTON • SYDNEY

For Max Louis Casling Simpson

First published 2000 by Walker Books Ltd
87 Vauxhall Walk, London SE11 5HJ

2 4 6 8 10 9 7 5 3 1

This book has been typeset in Plantin.

Printed in Great Britain by
St Edmundsbury Press, Bury St Edmunds

British Library Cataloguing in Publication Data
A catalogue record for this book is
available from the British Library.

ISBN 0-7445-5966-9

Contents

Chapter 1

The Locked Door

....

The distant sound of chanting grew:
children's voices repeating the same words
over and over again in a singsong rhythm.
Then suddenly the chanting faded and a
terrible sense of urgency took its place.

Sam tried to shout "Get out! Get out!" but
no sound came from his throat. There were
people rushing, rushing about in all
directions, people with red faces and red hair,
then suddenly he was leaping high into the
air. He woke with a jolt.

"Have I landed?" he murmured.

Then he woke up properly and smiled with
relief as he saw the tiny roof window and the
cosy attic room. He felt sure that he'd had the
same dream the night before, but it was hard
to be certain. Though it was daylight, the sun
wasn't streaming down through the window

as it had yesterday. It felt a bit chilly too, so he just lay there thinking and enjoying the softness and warmth of the narrow bed tucked neatly beneath the sloping ceiling.

It was the middle of a two-week Whitsun holiday in Whitby and Sam had reached the boredom stage. Sea, sand, seagulls and candy floss had gradually lost their appeal. He'd eaten so much fish and chips and fudge that he felt he'd burst. He'd been round the scary Dracula Experience, where waxwork vampires moved and moaned, giving terrible shocks and surprises. The whole family had been on the Ghost Walk, and Sam had been quite happy for once that his older sister Janet had clutched his arm tightly. They had crept around the old town in the dusk, listening to the storyteller's spooky tales.

Sam had been up and down the steep steps that led to the famous cliff-top abbey several times. There were supposed to be one hundred and ninety-nine steps, but each time he tried to count them, he got a different result.

Now, on this dull morning, he wasn't sure what to do next; he thought perhaps he'd done everything there was to do.

At last, hunger got the better of him. He slipped out of bed and walked downstairs. He passed his parents sitting at the dining-table, sipping coffee and reading newspapers. His sister Janet was looking bored and painting her nails.

When he pulled back the curtains above the small kitchen sink, he saw that a thick white mist was rolling in from the sea. "Huh!" he muttered. "Thought we were supposed to come here for the view!"

"Shut up!" Janet told him. "It's bad enough without you going on about it."

He could hardly see further than the little balcony of their holiday cottage on the end of Henrietta Street. There should have been a wonderful view of the harbour and lighthouses, but all was blank whiteness.

"What are we going to do?" he asked.

"Can't do anything in this." Janet pulled a face and started blowing on her nails, flapping her fingers about.

His parents ignored him and turned over more pages of their newspapers.

"That stuff stinks," Sam told his sister. He got a glass of milk from the fridge, and a slice of cold buttered toast, and took them back upstairs to his attic.

It was a little hole of a room, with its snug bed and not much else. Strong smells of smoking kippers drifted over from the kipper sheds across the street. The smell seemed to seep right through the walls, but it didn't bother Sam. He'd bagged the attic as soon as they arrived. Janet had raised her eyebrows in disgust. "You're welcome," she'd said. "I'd rather have the bigger one on the first floor, near Mum and Dad. It'll be spooky up here, all by yourself."

It was true that Sam had been having those disturbing dreams since sleeping there, but they hadn't exactly been scary, just filled with frantic rushing about. Sam himself was always running in the dream, though he didn't seem to know why. Sometimes strange whirring noises were there in the background and the sharp sound of chopping. Of course, there was the chanting too. He wished he could hear the words properly. If the dream ever came again, he'd try really hard to listen to those words.

He sighed with boredom and pulled aside the curtain of the cubby-hole that was used as a wardrobe. It was fitted with a clothes rail and hangers. He thought he might as well get wrapped up warm and go out in the mist by himself, seeing as Janet was being so annoying.

As he reached inside to grab his jacket, he saw something that he hadn't noticed before. The back of the cubby-hole wasn't just a plain old back, but a door, painted white to match the sides, with a worn wooden step up to it. The whole thing was made roughly like a shed door, with a sneck and keyhole and a thin strip of dark space showing at the top where it didn't fit very well. Above the door was a small plaster moulding of a face, with curly hair, two wings and a halo: an angel. It was unusual, because the angel had a rather thin face, not chubby like the usual cherubs. This plaster face was as thin as Sam's own and seemed somehow familiar.

He pushed the door, but it wouldn't give. Then he slipped his fingers into the space at the top and pulled it towards him. It rattled a bit but didn't open.

"Locked!" he whispered, disappointed.

Then suddenly he had another idea. He pulled his travel bag from beneath the bed, and fished inside until he found his torch. Grabbing the small three-legged stool that was the only other bit of furniture in the room, he dragged it towards the cupboard. Very carefully he pushed aside the few clothes that he'd bothered to hang up and pulled the stool in behind him.

It wobbled a bit as he stood on it and leant

forwards, but it was just the right height to allow him to shine his torch through the space at the top of the door and peep inside.

His heart beat fast as he aimed the beam of light down towards the ground, dreaming wildly of walled-up hidden treasure, or skeletons, perhaps a smugglers' hideaway. He slowly raised the light, sending spiders and beetles scuttling away into the cobwebs, and saw that it was just another narrow room, about the same size as his bedroom. It was full of dust and nothing else.

He got down from the stool, disappointed again. Well – at least it *was* a secret room. That was good and he wouldn't tell Janet about it, but it was a shame that it didn't have anything spooky or interesting in it. He sat down on the bed for a moment and switched off his torch; then he sighed, picked up his jacket and went downstairs.

Chapter 2

In the Mist

....

"I'm going out on the beach," Sam announced.

His parents nodded vaguely and returned to their newspapers and coffee cups, telling each other how wonderfully relaxed they felt. Sam began to think that going back to Sheffield at the end of the week might not be such a bad thing after all; at least he'd have friends there to do things with.

"Going out!" he repeated.

He stomped angrily down the steep steps that led to the beach, and wandered over the sands, up onto Tate Hill Pier. As seagulls swooped down out of the mist, crying like cats, he passed an old man slowly walking a little white dog. Nobody else seemed to be around, though it was hard to be sure when you couldn't see properly.

The sand beside the pier looked soft and

dry, even though the air was damp. He tried jumping off the edge of the pier where the drop was only a few feet. There was something quite satisfying about it, so he climbed back onto the pier and went a bit further along. The next jump was bigger and he landed with a thud. That felt even better.

He climbed back up and set off along the pier for a third time, walking past piles of stacked crab pots. Then dimly, in the distance, he saw the dark shapes of two people sitting on the seat near the end of the pier. They were dressed in black and sitting with their backs to him; both had long black hair and Sam couldn't help but stare. The darkness of their hair and clothes made sinister shadows among the soft white mist that surrounded them. It made him think of pictures that he'd seen in the Dracula Experience. They sat there quietly as though admiring the view, but all the thick whiteness rolling about them meant that they couldn't even see to the other side of the harbour.

It looked pretty weird!

Then suddenly it happened, the awful thing. The man turned round and looked at Sam; his face was deathly white, with dark red lips and great purple shadows above his eyes. He smiled and Sam suddenly saw the gleaming sharp tips of long pointed teeth.

"Help," he muttered. "Dracula!"

Staggering backwards, he half fell, half jumped off the pier. He went with such force that he sprawled in the sand.

The dark figure that had given Sam such a shock got up from his seat and ran along the pier towards him. He leapt down onto the sands, his wide black cape floating out behind him. A young woman rushed after him; she was wearing a long, trailing, purple dress, her face as white and weird as his.

Sam just lay there and closed his eyes for a moment. Was this another terrible dream?

"I'm so sorry. Didn't mean to startle you like that." A polite and concerned-sounding voice spoke to him. "Are you OK?"

Sam opened his eyes. All at once he felt foolish. When he looked properly at them he saw that they were just a young man and woman who were dressed in strange clothes and wearing rather stunning make-up.

"Oh," he said, struggling to get up. "I thought – I thought you were..."

"No!" the girl giggled. "We're goths. We just like dressing up – that's all."

The young man grasped Sam by the hand and hauled him to his feet.

"Well – if you're sure that you're all right?"

"Fine – I'm fine." Sam nodded.

The goth lady tucked her hand into the young man's arm. They turned away, waving and heading up the steps towards Church Street. Sam stood there feeling foolish, seeing dimly through the mist that a girl about his own age was sitting on the edge of the pier, watching it all and grinning.

He felt so stupid.

"Have you never seen goths before?" she asked.

Sam wasn't sure that he had, so he said nothing.

"It's going to be a special goth weekend," the girl told him chattily. "Whitby will be packed full of them over the next few days."

Before Sam had chance to answer, there was a cackle of laughter from behind him that made him jump again. It was the old man who'd been walking his dog.

"It's not goths you want to worry about," he said. "And it's not Dracula either. It's red devils! Whitby was packed full of them once and their holes are still here! Everywhere!"

"Mr Barker, you're a red devil yourself!" the girl shouted cheekily after him.

The old man didn't seem insulted, just wandered off laughing again, leaving Sam feeling a bit shivery.

"Want a cup of tea?" the young girl offered. "You can come to Mam's tea room. She'll be opening up now and she'll be glad of a customer; there won't be many today."

Sam felt in his pockets; a cup of tea

sounded good. "Haven't brought any money with me."

The girl sighed. "One free cup," she said, very businesslike. "Mam will give you one free cup, then you'll have to pay next time."

So that was how Sam found himself sitting in an empty café on a very foggy morning with a talkative Whitby girl called Naomi.

"Any cakes?" Naomi looked hopefully at her mother.

Naomi's mother smiled and clicked her tongue. "Eee! Dear! We're not going to make our fortune this way," she said, but she brought a plate of warm flapjacks along with two steaming cups of tea.

When they'd finished eating and drinking Sam felt much better, but he sat there quietly, wondering if he should leave now and go back to Henrietta Street.

"Naomi!" her mother called. "I could do with a few pots washing, honey!"

Naomi pulled a face and got up from her

seat. "I'll do it later," she called back. "I've got to show this boy the way!"

"What? I know the way," he told her. He didn't want her thinking he was that stupid.

"Doesn't matter," Naomi hissed. "Just get me out of here."

Then Sam understood. He'd do the same himself if his mother started talking about washing pots. He nodded, got up and went out of the café with her.

Chapter 3

On Tate Hill Sands

Small patches of sunlight cut down through
the mist and the morning seemed to brighten
as Sam and Naomi walked down the cobbled
street and found themselves back on Tate Hill
Sands. Without saying anything else, Naomi
started strolling along beside the tide line,
looking intently at the damp marked sand.
The sea had left masses of seaweed, pebbles
and rubbish there.

"What're you looking for?" Sam asked her.

She shrugged her shoulders. "Anything,"
she said. "Shells, stones, jet, driftwood. I
found a pair of good sunglasses once and an
old gold watch. Jet's best. I can take it to Mr
Barker and he'll give me money for it."

"What does he do with it?" Sam asked.

"He's a jet carver, silly. He makes it into
jewellery and sells it."

"Oh – I'll look," Sam told her. "What's it like?"

"Black and shining if it's sea washed."

"Here." Sam dived for a lump of gleaming black stone and handed it to her.

"Nah." She shook her head disgustedly. "That's just coal – it's everywhere."

Sam sighed and threw it down. If shiny black coal was everywhere, finding jet must be pretty difficult.

As Sam and Naomi wandered further down the beach, past the holiday cottages, Sam kept glancing up at the terraces. They appeared ghostlike from the mist high above and topped a huge bank of boulders which protected the crumbly headland from the sea. Sam went striding ahead over rockpools.

"You want to be careful," Naomi suggested, just as Sam suddenly slithered full-length into a deep rock pool.

"Flipping heck!" he growled. This was obviously going to be a day for making a fool of himself. His jeans were soaked and the water was surprisingly cold.

Naomi sighed again and shook her head. "You'll have to go and get changed," she told him. "You ought to have a hot bath too."

"Who does she think she is?" Sam muttered. "My mother?"

He glanced down as he scrambled awkwardly out of the water and saw a glistening black lump wedged deep in the pool, between two rocks. He was already sopping wet, so he plunged his hand in again and pulled the black lump out of the crevice.

"I suppose this'll be coal, too," he said, emerging from the water and dripping all over the sand.

Naomi took the black shining lump from him and held it close to her face, frowning. Then she threw it gently up and down in her hand as though weighing it. "Might be the real thing," she said reluctantly. "And it's a big piece too."

"Really?" Sam stared down at the black lump that had felt so light when he'd picked it up. Surely this couldn't be the treasure that Naomi was looking for; he always thought of valuable stuff as being heavy, like gold.

"You'd better run back to your place and get changed," Naomi told him, sounding even more like his mother. "Run straight back, or you'll catch your death of cold. Go on, don't stand about."

Sam's teeth were beginning to chatter and he could see the sense in what she said, so he started to trudge back to the holiday home. He climbed the steep steps, and just as he reached the top one he stopped for a moment. "She's blooming well got my lump of jet!" he muttered. His cold wet jeans chafed at his knees, making him feel so uncomfortable that he couldn't face the thought of going back to ask for it, so he just pushed open the sliding door and stumbled inside.

Naomi watched carefully from the beach to see which house he went into.

*   *   *

"What on earth?" said Janet as he rushed, dripping, through the living space and headed upstairs.

His mother put down her newspaper and followed him. "Samuel?" she said. "Have you been in the sea?" When she saw the state of him, she stopped fussing, grabbed a towel and led him back to the bathroom. "Hot bath," she insisted. And Sam didn't argue with that.

A good soak in hot water had never seemed so pleasant, though he felt a little sad that his peculiar adventure seemed to suddenly have come to an end. He supposed it would be back to boredom and baiting Janet now. When at last he felt thoroughly warmed through again, he got dressed in the fresh clothes that his mother had put out for him, thinking that he heard a bit of a commotion downstairs.

Janet stomped up the stairs looking disgusted. "You've got a visitor," she said. "There's some girl asking for you."

Sam grinned. "Naomi?" he whispered. Suddenly he knew that it wasn't all over, not yet – there was much, much more to do. He pulled on his stiff damp trainers and went downstairs. Naomi was sitting on the sofa, looking a bit uncomfortable and surprisingly shy.

"Hi!" he said.

"Hi!" she replied.

There was a moment of awkward silence before she picked up the black lump from her lap. "Do you want to find out if it's really jet?" she asked.

"Of course."

"Got a pin?"

They all looked around puzzled for a moment before Sam's mother got up and went to her bag. "I've got a needle," she said. "I keep it in the first-aid box."

"That'll do," Naomi agreed.

They all watched, rather impressed, as Naomi pressed hard with the needle and made a small scratch on the black shape.

"Yes!" she breathed. "Look at that. See that ginger-coloured powder coming out of the scratch? I think it really is jet. If it was coal, that would be black."

"Is it worth something?" Janet was interested now.

Naomi nodded. "It might be. We'd have to ask Mr Barker to be sure."

Chapter 4

Finders Keepers

....

Sam and Naomi walked along Church Street,
turning off into a quiet alleyway called
Barker's Yard. It was full of cottages
crammed together, some big, some tiny. The
jet man lived in one of them. Naomi reached
up to open a high side gate that enclosed a
small garden and work shed.

"Now then, Mr Barker," she called.

"Will he mind?" Sam asked.

"Course not!" Naomi grinned. "His bark is
worse than his bite! Get it?"

"What?" Sam frowned.

"Get it?" Naomi insisted. "Mr Barker?"

"Oh!" Sam sighed, feeling really stupid
again. "Yes – I get it."

"That you, lass?" a familiar crackly voice
called out. Sam remembered that Mr Barker
was the old man who'd been walking his dog

on the beach. He'd laughed and said something rather scary about Whitby being full of devils. Sam wasn't at all sure that he wanted to meet him again, but Naomi opened the door and gave him a shove.

"Go on in," she said.

Sam found himself in a small workshop that smelled of turpentine and linseed. It was quite cosy inside, with a coal-fired stove glowing in the corner and an old-fashioned kettle bubbling away on the top. The small white dog jumped up at them both, yapping with pleasure and wagging his tail.

"Now then, Snowy," said Naomi, scratching the silky ears.

"I don't know how you manage it, my lass," the old man said, teasing. "You always turn up just when I'm going to make tea."

"That's because you are always making tea," said Naomi.

"Come on, lad, sit down," Mr Barker told Sam. "I daresay you won't say no to a cup of tea and a ginger biscuit."

"Thanks," Sam agreed, shyly.

Sam sipped his tea, nibbled his biscuit and stared about him. A modern-looking lathe stood on a workbench along with other equipment that put him in mind of the dentist's. Lumps of brownish-blue stone had been sorted into different sizes and piled up in the corner. Beautiful gleaming old-fashioned black brooches and pairs of dainty earrings lay in little boxes on another bench on the far side.

"Show him what you found," Naomi insisted.

"Aye – now then, let me see," the old man said, getting a magnifying glass down from the shelf. He took the black lump into his hand, jiggling it carefully up and down. "Weight's right!" he agreed. "Let's have a look."

There was a moment of quietness while he examined it carefully.

"Is it jet?" Naomi was impatient.

"It is," he agreed. "Look here," he said,

giving the magnifying glass to Sam. "Can you see those lines?"

Sam saw only a blur at first, then as he moved the magnifying glass closer a neat pattern of wavy lines fell into place. "Yes," he said, amazed. "I can. They're like the rings you see on trees, when they've been cut down."

"That's it exactly." Mr Barker was pleased with him. "Millions of years ago this lump of jet was part of a living tree. Araucaria, they call it, something like the spiky monkey-puzzle tree we have today."

"Wow!" Sam breathed. "Does it all come from the sea?"

The old man shook his head and picked up a bluish-brown lump from the workbench. "This is rough jet from the cliffs at Boulby," he said. "My dad used to go searching for it up there."

"Tell him about the ropes," Naomi said. She'd clearly heard this many times before.

Mr Barker smiled and shook his head. "He

wasn't a red devil, he were a dare-devil, my dad. He used to let himself down the cliff face on a rope and dangle there high above the sea, seagulls flapping about him, huge waves bashing below. He'd be there, chiselling away, getting the best hard jet. Then he'd come hauling himself back up with a bag full of good pieces on his back."

"Dangerous!" Sam whispered.

"Oh aye. There were terrible accidents; some of them that did it fell and got badly hurt, some were killed."

There was silence for a moment.

"Did you say something about red devils?" Sam asked, remembering how the old man had laughed down on the beach.

Mr Barker laughed again, but it sounded friendlier this time. "I was just having a bit of a joke with you," he said. "Red devils – Whitby was full of them. They were the rouge men, who worked on the polishing wheels. They used jeweller's rouge and oil and it gave the jet a lovely velvety finish, but the oily mixture covered the men with red paste. Their hair, their clothes, their hands and faces were all red."

"So they called them red devils?" Sam said, relieved. But then suddenly he remembered his dream and his heart skipped a beat. "Red hands, and hair and faces," he murmured.

"Aye. You want to go down to the Victorian Jet Works at the bottom of Church Street," Mr Barker told him. "They'll tell you what life was like for the jet carvers who lived here in Whitby, about a hundred years ago."

Naomi picked up the piece of jet. "Are you going to pay us for it?" she asked.

Mr Barker shook his head, unsure. "It's a good-sized piece, but look here and here. It's got two cracks in it. As soon as you start to work it, that's going to split into three."

They looked carefully where he pointed and could see what he meant.

"I might give you a few pounds for it," he said. "But you're maybe best to keep it – keep it as a souvenir of Whitby town. There's no better souvenir than a piece of jet that you've found yourself."

Mr Barker handed the gleaming black lump back to Sam. It sat there warm and satisfying in the palm of his hand.

"Jet's supposed to be magical," Mr Barker added. "Meant to bring good luck to those who find it."

Sam grinned. He hesitated for a moment, then held it out to Naomi. "You can have it," he said. "You were the one who was looking for it."

But Naomi shook her head. "No. Finders keepers," she said. "It belongs to you."

Chapter 5

Dreaming of Jet

....

Sam was exhausted by the time he got to bed
that night. He put down the precious piece of
jet next to his bedside lamp, and fell asleep at
once.

At first he slept peacefully, but then one of
those strange dreams began. First of all he
heard the chanting, then everything seemed
to change again and suddenly he was
hurrying, hurrying like mad. He felt that he'd
got to do something that was really important
and he'd got to do it fast, but he couldn't
quite remember what it was.

Then he was woken by the whirring of
machinery and sharp bangs like the sound of
a butcher chopping meat. The chanting had
faded and instead he could hear low
murmuring voices.

Sam opened his eyes to find that his small

attic room was quite light. At first he thought he must have left the cubby-hole light switch on, for the low spreading glow seemed to come from inside it.

He sat up in bed and put out his hand towards the lamp, but instead of finding the plastic switch his hand touched his piece of jet. Sam gasped and pulled his hand sharply away; it was warm to the touch – really warm.

His stomach churned for a moment, but then he smiled, telling himself that he must be dreaming again and this was really quite a funny dream and not scary. He put out his hand again and picked the jet up; it felt warm as a person might feel – almost as though alive. Well, the old man had said that it might be magical and bring luck.

Clutching the jet in his hand, Sam wriggled out of his bedclothes and slid down the bed. As he got closer to the glowing light inside the cubby-hole, he realized that it was flickering, as though the bulb was about to go, or perhaps not quite fitted properly into

the socket. He stretched his hand out and
began to pull back the curtain, but what he
saw inside the wardrobe made his heart
thump very fast.

His clothes were there, just where he'd left
them, hanging up and pushed to the side, but
the flickering light came from beyond the rail.
The locked door was standing wide open,
and whirring sounds and voices came from
the room beyond the step. The flickering
light was not in the cupboard at all, but it
came from candles that lit the small room
above.

Sam's mouth dropped open and, though he
hung on tight to his magical lump of jet, his
hands shook violently.

He glimpsed a dusty room crammed with
busy working men. Old-fashioned cocoa and
cigarette advertisements decorated the walls,
and though the sun was setting you could see
dark pink sky through the roof windows
above, and snow – he could see snow drifting
down. A boy no older than himself was sitting

carving a lump of light brown stone, quite close to him on the step.

"Oh help!" Sam whispered.

The boy suddenly looked up and saw him; his mouth dropped open with surprise. It was too much for Sam; he dropped the lump of jet and it landed with a bang. There was sudden silence, black darkness fell everywhere. He turned round and leapt back towards his bed. This dream was getting far too real for comfort. He scrambled quickly back and hid under the bedclothes.

Everything stayed quiet as he lay there. He wondered if there'd be a sudden terrifying thump on his bed, but nothing came. After what seemed ages he began to feel silly. Of course it was only a dream – it must have been. He wriggled out of the bedclothes, sat up and clicked on the bedside lamp. All was still and quiet. The curtain that covered the front of the makeshift wardrobe had been pulled open, but otherwise everything looked normal – no light on inside it.

"Stupid! I must have been out of bed and sleepwalking," he murmured. He left the bedside lamp on and snuggled down again, settling quickly back to sleep.

When he woke in the morning Sam found his room bright with sunlight. He got out of bed and ran downstairs to pull open the curtains above the sink. It was a wonderful morning, without a trace of fog or mist. He could see right across the harbour, past the lighthouses and along the curving coastline to Sandsend. Fishing boats were ploughing steadily home after a night at sea, followed by hordes of wheeling seagulls, screeching for a fish head or a tail. Distant headlands stood out clear and solid against the blue sky, and an oil-tanker moved slowly along the horizon.

He sighed with satisfaction. "What a good morning! What a crazy night!" he murmured.

He went back upstairs and looked inside the wardrobe cupboard. There was the door, just as he'd seen it the first time, closed. He reached inside and gave it a push. Of course it was firmly locked and just rattled a bit. Then as he moved back, his foot caught something on the floor. It was the piece of jet, smashed cleanly into three pieces.

Sam stooped sadly to pick them up. How right Mr Barker had been! Still, they were quite nice little bits, just about big enough for brooches, if only he could manage to carve them.

He put them back on the shelf beside the lamp and went down to get some breakfast. He wouldn't waste time; Naomi had told him to call for her and she'd insisted that she'd go with him to the Victorian Jet Works.

His family were surprised when he refused to go with them to Saltburn for the day. "There's a lovely wide beach there, just perfect on a sunny day like this," his mother told him. "Will you be OK here by yourself?"

"I'll be with Naomi," he told them.

"I think you'd better go and live with Naomi," Janet sneered.

"Be quiet, miss," Dad told her firmly. "It's good that he's made friends and that he's enjoying his holiday."

Chapter 6

Jettie Lads Are Dirty

....

Sam was beginning to think that it must be quite good to live above a café. Naomi's mother gave him another cup of tea and a bun, and still didn't ask him to pay for it. He told them how his jet had got broken. "I was sleepwalking," he said. "And having a funny dream."

"I said you were daft," Naomi giggled.

"Let's have some manners, Naomi!" Her mother frowned. Then she said kindly to Sam, "Don't you worry, honey! I should think it's sleeping in a strange bed that's causing those dreams. Though Whitby folk have always believed that there is something magical about jet. My mother could remember Whitby being full of jettie lads when she was very small." She looked thoughtful for a moment and laughed. "She told me that the lasses used to tease them by singing a song as they skipped in the street. Now how did it go?"

Naomi sighed, and looked embarrassed. "Oh, don't start singing, Mam."

But her mother was enjoying herself now and she started clapping and tapping her foot, chanting:

"Sailor lads are fair of face,
And fisher lads are bonny,
But jettie lads are dirty lads,
A-making of their money.

Jettie lads are dirty lads,
From eight-year-old to thirty,
They sit like fools in piles of dust,
And that's what makes them dirty!"

As she sang the old song a shiver ran down Sam's back. From the moment she began he knew he'd heard this song somewhere before, then all at once he realized. "That song – it was in my dream," he said.

Naomi laughed and shook her head. "You are daft."

Sam was quite sure that this was the chanting that he'd heard. He'd tried to listen and catch the words while he was sleeping, but they'd never been clear enough. Things from his dream seemed to be cropping up all the time, and it almost seemed as though he was getting answers to questions without even having to ask. It was all very strange, but now he knew those words he'd never forget them.

Naomi's mother looked a bit concerned. "Are you all right, honey?" she asked. "You've gone a bit pale."

"He needs some fresh air," Naomi insisted. "Come on, we were going to go out anyway."

Goths wandered up and down Church Street in bright sunshine, dressed in wild and fantastic clothes, looking in all the little shops. It was like a fancy dress parade.

"I wish they'd make jet jewellery for goths," one of the girls murmured as she stared into a shop window.

"It would be a great day for being on the beach," Sam said to Naomi as they marched up Church Street yet again. "I don't think I really like museums much."

"You'll like this one," Naomi told him firmly, and she turned out to be right.

It was a tiny place, and when you went in you couldn't imagine how you'd spend much time there. The front was like a small shop and the man who sat at the desk looked up and raised his eyebrows when he saw Naomi.

"Hi, Harry!" she said. She seemed to know everyone in Whitby by name.

"Hi there, Naomi!" he replied. "And what have you come for? Haven't you seen enough of our little jet works?"

"I have, but he hasn't," Naomi told him. She pushed Sam forward bossily. "Show him the workshop and tell him all about it."

Harry looked thoughtfully at Sam for a moment. "Now then, lad," he asked, his voice deep and dramatic like an actor's. "What is it that you have come for?"

Sam was puzzled. For a moment he wished he hadn't come at all, and he wondered if he dare walk straight out again. Then he remembered his beautiful piece of jet, now broken into three lumps. "I want to know about jet!" he answered determinedly.

"Excellent." Harry beamed. "You've come to the right place. You see, we know quite a lot about how the Victorian jet workers made the beautiful things that you can still see up in Pannett Park Museum. People have studied the subject and written books about it, but what we've got hidden away behind the curtains at the back of our shop is something more. It's evidence. Real evidence!"

Sam smiled. Listening to Harry talk was rather like listening to a story.

"Now then, when you want to know the

real truth about something, you must always ask for evidence." Harry banged his fist on the table, making them both jump. "Evidence! Evidence is what you need!"

Sam nodded in agreement.

Harry continued his story, telling how, about ten years ago, a builder had bought an old house in Whitby and decided to do it up, to make it into holiday flats. He'd started on the cellar and worked slowly upwards through the house, dividing rooms, putting in bathrooms and fixing the whole place up. At last he got right up to a tiny attic room, but when he stripped away old boarding from one of the walls, he found something very surprising indeed behind it.

Sam's stomach gave a lurch. He tried to speak but couldn't think what to say; he had a peculiar feeling that he knew what was coming next.

"What's up?" Naomi asked.

"Is my story boring you?" Harry asked.

Sam shook his head like mad. "No," he

insisted. "Tell me … please tell me. What was it that the man found behind the boards?"

"There was a wooden step and a door."

"A locked door?" Sam could hardly breathe.

Harry frowned and shook his head. "No. I don't think so; he just opened the door and walked into a complete and perfect little jet workshop. Everything was there: the grinding wheels, the polishing wheels, the handmade carving tools, even the workmen's coats hanging up on pegs. It was just as if they'd walked out of it the day before."

Chapter 7

Straight Into a Dream

Sam was trembling with excitement. Everything that Harry said seemed to confirm his suspicions about the tiny attic room that he slept in, and the dream that kept coming back again and again. He was bursting with questions, but didn't know what to ask first.

"Why would they have just stopped work and left it like that?"

Harry shrugged his shoulders. "Well, that's a bit of a mystery," he said. "When Queen Victoria's husband died, all the rich London people started wearing black clothes, and they wore black jewellery too."

"They wore jet?" Sam asked.

"That's right. It became so fashionable that everyone wanted to wear it. The money to be earned from carving jet shot sky-high. People in Whitby left other work to set up jet workshops in their attics and sorting shops in their back rooms and cellars."

"Only in Whitby?"

"Whitby jet is the best you can get," Naomi told him.

"She's right." Harry nodded. "The jet industry boomed here in Whitby, but as it became more and more popular, cheap imitations were brought in from elsewhere. Then, when the court came out of mourning, everyone wanted bright colours instead. Suddenly the market dropped; nobody wanted it any more. Jettie lads were starving on the streets and you couldn't sell a jet workshop for love nor money. Now that might have been why it was boarded up and left there in the attic."

"Perhaps the owner got ill or even died," Naomi suggested. "His wife might have been so sad that she just covered it all up."

"That's quite possible too," Harry agreed.

"I wish I could see it," said Sam. "Do you

think it had young jettie lads working in it?"

"Oh yes," said Harry. "Jettie lads would start work as young as eight or nine. And you can see it, if you want to." Harry got up and came round his desk. "That's what we've got hidden away behind our bead curtain."

"That workshop? The real one?" Sam couldn't believe it.

Harry nodded. "It couldn't stay up there in the attic, so it was brought down here and set up again. Though it's not in quite the right place, at least it meant that it could be saved and people could come to look at it. Want to see it now?"

Sam swallowed hard. "Yes, please!"

Harry went over to the back of the shop and held open the beaded curtain so that they could all go through. Sam walked straight into his dream.

It was all there: the wheels, the tools, the roof windows, the cocoa and cigarette advertisements decorating the walls. Dark ginger-coloured dust was everywhere. The only things missing were the men and the noise and that boy.

Sam stared about him.

"Good, isn't it?" said Harry. "It was found somewhere up—"

Sam couldn't stop himself from butting in. "Henrietta Street," he said. "They found it on Henrietta Street."

"That's right." Harry nodded, surprised.

"How did you know?" Naomi asked.

Sam shook his head. "I think it might – just might – have been the house where we're staying. Number 45."

"Well." Harry looked thoughtful. "I don't think that I've ever found out which number it was. I wasn't here myself when it all happened."

"It was number 45. I'm sure of it," said Sam.

Though the workshop was tiny, Sam felt as though he could have stayed there all day listening to Harry's stories. He heard how the young jettie lads were often put on grinding wheels and terrible accidents happened when the grinding wheels cracked or exploded.

"The records tell it all," said Harry. "William Locker killed – eighteen years old. Joseph Haxton killed – seventeen years old. William Easton – only sixteen." Harry picked up a small tin with a scraping of red powder in it. "Jeweller's rouge," he said.

"Red devils!" Sam told him.

"That's right," Harry agreed.

They stayed for an hour and they would have stayed longer except that a school party came crowding in with their teacher, wanting Harry to show them round and talk to them. A girl called Gemma had found some fossils in a shiny black lump on the beach.

"We wondered if it was jet?" she asked.

Harry took it and went to get his magnifying glass. "Evidence … evidence!" he muttered. Sam and Naomi went quietly out, leaving them to it.

They wandered back to Naomi's mother's

café and had a sandwich and lemonade for their lunch, then called in on Mr Barker to ask him if he wanted Snowy taking out for a walk.

He told them it would be grand to have Snowy walked a bit and asked if they'd been to the Victorian Jet Works.

"We have," Naomi told him. "Sam thinks that it's the house he's staying in where the workshop was found."

"Does he now?" Mr Barker looked surprised.

"It's number 45," said Sam. "And there's a little locked-up room in the attic, where I'm sleeping. There's nothing in it, just piles of dust."

"Well now." The old man scratched his head. "I think you may be right, lad. I believe it could well have been number 45. It was one of the ones right up at the end – one of the few left standing."

"Left standing?" Sam asked, puzzled.

"After the landslip," Mr Barker said.

"There was a terrible landslip up there in the year 1870, a freezing cold winter's night. The marvellous thing about it was that nobody died. Somebody seemed to have realized what was happening and gave a good warning. Still, it was a very bad thing. People were made homeless, and jet workshops all fell down into the sea – there were many businesses lost. No insurance like there is now. Oh dear yes ... Henrietta Street used to be twice as long as it is now."

Chapter 8

Going Crazy!

....

They walked on Tate Hill Sands, letting
Snowy off his lead, laughing at the way he
jumped into the edge of the sea. It was a
gorgeous sunny day and jolly music drifted
over from the bandstand on the other side of
the harbour. It was a perfect day for being on
a beach with a friendly girl and a funny little
dog, but somehow Sam couldn't get the
locked attic door out of his mind.

"Keep thinking," he said. "Thinking about
that locked door, up in my bedroom."

Naomi grinned. "I'd like to see it," she
said.

Sam held Snowy while Naomi climbed onto
the stool inside the cubby-hole, holding the
torch. "Wow!" she whispered.

"Well?" he asked. "What do you think?"

"Yes," she agreed. "I think you could be right. It's just … sort of disappointing somehow. Disappointing that it's empty – nothing there but dust."

Sam nodded. He knew what she meant, but when he thought about his dream, a feeling of excitement grew. It wasn't always empty. His dream had felt like something more than just an empty room – much more. Would it happen again? People did have dreams that came back, again and again. Though he was having a good time with Naomi and Snowy, he couldn't wait till the night came.

His parents and Janet came back from Saltburn looking pink and worn out.

"Oh, you don't know what you've missed," Janet told him. "Lads on surfboards everywhere. Just like *Home and Away*!"

After their evening meal, everyone seemed to want to go to bed early, and Sam was perfectly happy about that. He lay in his bed, trying hard to get to sleep. He sighed and rolled about. "Oh why," he muttered, "why is it that just when you want to go to sleep, you can't? How did it happen last time?" he asked himself.

Then he remembered that it had been something to do with the jet. The jet had turned warm in his hands, and when he'd dropped it, suddenly everything vanished. It was almost as if the jet had somehow taken him into the dream. Where had he left it? He sat up in bed and put the light on.

It was there, right beside his lamp, three small pieces. He put out his hand and touched it. Nothing! It wasn't cold, but then he knew that jet never did feel really cold. He must be going crazy. Naomi was right to call him daft! He clicked off the lamp, but then as he pulled his hand away he brushed against something warm. It was the jet, and it had turned noticeably warm in a split second. There was something else too – though he'd turned off his lamp, the room wasn't dark;

the gentle flickering of candlelight came from inside the cubby-hole once again.

Sam carefully picked up his three warm pieces of jet – two in one hand, one in the other. It was the jet that brought this magic, he had no doubt of that, and he somehow knew that he must keep the pieces with him. He carefully dropped each bit into the top pocket of his pyjamas, where he could feel them there, warm against his heart. They were new pyjamas that his mother had bought for him at Saltburn; bright red and fleecy. He'd thought them a bit girly when he'd first seen them, but now in the middle of the night he was glad of their warmth.

He crawled down to the bottom of his bed and pulled back the curtain and his heart skipped a beat as he saw that the door was standing wide open, just as before.

This time all the wheels in the workshop were still and for a moment he thought that there was nobody there. Then he saw the young boy, all alone, moving backwards and forwards across the space. He was sweeping up dust as little bits of plaster drifted down from the attic roof.

Sam ducked beneath the clothes rail and put his foot on the step. Just at that moment the sweeping boy looked straight at him. "Ah, it's thee again," he said. "I saw thee before and tha vanished. Gave me a right scare."

Sam brought his other foot up onto the step; suddenly he was there, standing barefoot in the workshop with the boy.

"Now that's a fine suit for a red devil." The boy stared at Sam's pyjamas. "That'll not show the rouge. Tha's not a real devil I hope, jumping out on me like that, coming from nowhere!"

Sam laughed and shook his head.

"Aye," the boy grinned. "But – tha's so clean! What's thee got in tha pocket?"

Sam carefully pulled out the jet to show him.

"That's three good brooch pieces you've got there."

"Yes," said Sam. "I wish I could carve them."

"I could show thee," the boy said eagerly. He stopped sweeping and held out his hand. "I'm Reuben Turner, jettie lad."

Sam shook him by the hand, feeling the roughness of the boy's work-hardened fingers.

"They give me nowt but soapstone to carve," the boy insisted. "They leave me to sweep up and keep watch, but one day I'll surprise them. It will say Reuben Turner outside these works and I'll be a fine jet carver like my dad."

"I'm sure you will," Sam agreed, wondering if he dare make a suggestion.

"Tha's the first one that's had faith in me," Reuben said, pleased and surprised.

"I've got complete faith in you," Sam told him. "And – I know this may sound a bit strange – if you get old and cannot work any more, or if a time comes when you cannot get good money for your jet, will you leave your workshop here? Will you board it all up, so that it stays here, a secret in this attic?"

Reuben Turner stared. "That's a rum idea," he said. "I don't know about that! I cannot believe that folks will ever not want jet! But, as for now, I could help thee make those pieces into fine name brooches. What names would thee want?"

"Oh, um, Naomi," he said. "And Janet, I suppose."

"What else?"

"Don't know." Sam shrugged.

Chapter 9

Much More
Than a Dream

Reuben finished his sweeping and put the brush neatly to one side.

"I'd help you to carve those name brooches for nowt," he said. "I'd do it just to get some practice on three good little pieces of jet."

"I'd like that," said Sam. "But I've got to keep hold of them, just at the moment."

"Fair enough," the boy agreed. He picked up a bundle of what looked like roughly made old-fashioned pens, with the holders all wrapped about with rags. "Now then, I shall let you use my carving tools on a bit of soapstone," he told Sam.

Sam nodded, aware that he was being honoured. "Where are all the other men?" he asked.

"Oh, they'll be in their beds by now," Reuben told him. "I've to clean up and then keep watch. Does thee want to stay? I could do with the company – and I'll get thee carving a bit. Gets terrible boring up here. I'm always falling asleep."

Reuben blew out three guttering candles and pinched the smoking wicks with care; then he took up the fourth and carried it past Sam, starting down the steps. Sam was nervous about turning round and looking back into the cubby-hole and his own little room, unsure of what he'd see. There was nothing for it but to do it. He took a deep breath and swung round.

"Oh my goodness!" he breathed.

The cubby-hole had vanished and a narrow, rather grubby-looking mattress lay on the floor in the place where his bed usually was, the walls covered in dull peeling plaster. A chipped bowl and water jug and a plate with a hunk of bread and a kipper on it stood on the floor beside the mattress.

"Ah, some things don't change," Sam whispered.

Apart from that, the room was empty and it felt very cold indeed. There seemed to be nothing to do but follow Reuben to his bed on the floor and crouch there beside him, trying to keep warm.

"Are you watching for robbers?" he asked.

"Aye, maybe robbers, but mostly fires."

"Could do with a bit of a fire," Sam muttered.

"Phew ... we'd have the whole place going up in a flash," Reuben insisted. "Gets set on fire very easily, does jet. Didn't you know that? Here," he said, pulling a piece of light brown stone from his pocket. "Soapstone to practise on." Then he took a sharp, pointed tool from the bundle. "Have a go with this. Just practise digging out small rounds. You can make a fine spotty pattern once you've got the knack of it."

"What's it made from?" Sam stared down doubtfully at the small tool.

"Sharpened umbrella spoke," Reuben told him. "Best thing to start with, is that."

Sam gripped the rag-bound handle and tried. The rough-made tool did seem to work quite well and the rags on the handle stopped it slipping. He dug away while Reuben poured water from the jug and then dipped his hands in and out of the bowl so fast that Sam knew the water was as cold as the attic room.

"It's working," he cried, delighted with the spotty pattern that was developing on the stone.

"Not bad, not bad," Reuben agreed. He dried himself quickly on a rag, then tucked into his kipper and bread, using his hands to peel the skin carefully away. "Want a bit?" he asked.

"No," said Sam, engrossed in his carving, then added, "thank you very much."

Reuben ate in silence for a moment or two.

"Freezing for Whit holidays, isn't it," Sam murmured.

Reuben chewed thoughtfully for a moment, then he shook his head. "Thee's got tha holidays mixed up," he said. "Soon be Christmas holiday – thee can't have forgotten that."

Sam looked up at Reuben, puzzled, and as he watched him picking carefully at the kipper bones he remembered that he'd seen snow floating down onto the roof window the first time that he'd been here.

He looked upwards, but could see nothing but darkness through the small window. Then, instead of snow, he saw a rather large flake of plaster drift down from the ceiling. A faint but terrible suspicion came into his mind, but it seemed so ridiculous that he pushed it away again.

"Did you see that?" he asked Reuben. "Plaster falling down from the roof?"

"That's nowt." Reuben shrugged his shoulders. "Plaster's always falling round here. It's the shaking of the wheels that causes it, all these workshops crammed into the roofs."

They were quiet again, but Sam couldn't

forget what Mr Barker had told him. "How many houses on Henrietta Street?" he asked.

Reuben looked up, amazed. "I don't know … tha'd best go and count them! Maybe ninety – or even a hundred."

Sam put down the soapstone and the umbrella spoke tool; something much more urgent was preying on his mind. He got to his feet. "I've got to go outside," he said suddenly.

"Oh aye." Reuben thought that he'd understood. "Go downstairs, the privy's round the back."

Sam walked shaky legged down bare boarded stairs, not caring that his feet were now numb with cold. He came out onto the street in near darkness; just the faint flickering of lights in the house windows showed that Henrietta Street stretched away towards the cliff edge as far as he could see. He stood there, seagulls wheeling and crying as they always did, but then he heard crackling. It sounded as though a small amount of gritty shale had come sliding down from the upper cliffs, looming high above the houses.

"Oh no," he whispered. "Oh help. This is more than a dream, much more, and I've chosen the wrong moment to be here." What was it that Mr Barker had said? Lots of houses sliding into the sea, but … nobody killed. He was sure the old jet carver had said that nobody had been killed.

Chapter 10

Not a Devil

....

Remembering that nobody had died calmed
Sam down a little, but then he held his breath
as a gentle, trembling sensation rose from the
ground beneath his feet. It was so slight that
he couldn't be certain about it; perhaps it was
just his own body shivering with cold. It
stopped and Sam breathed again, but then he
saw something that really frightened him – a
dark crack in the dirt road in front of him.

It wasn't anything dramatic, just a thin
black wavy line and hard to see, but he felt
sure that it couldn't have been there before.
Then another trickle of shale rolled down
from the cliffs and clattered into somebody's
backyard, so that all the seagulls squawked
like mad and fled out to sea.

Sam waited for the people to come spilling
out of their houses, but just one old man

came from his front door, dressed in a long nightshirt. He looked down past the side of his house, where the sprinkling of shale had landed.

"Look out!" Sam told him. "The cliffs are going to come rumbling down."

"What? Nay, lad. 'Tis nowt but a trickle. You'll not get me running out of my home for that!"

Sam stared aghast as the old man hobbled back into his house and shut the door. He couldn't believe it. They were all just staying there, tucked up in their beds. His heart began to thump uncomfortably. What was he to do? Didn't Mr Barker say that somebody had raised the alarm? But nobody was doing it. He didn't like the thought at all, but he began to realize that perhaps he would have to do it himself.

He hesitated for a moment, thinking that he might have got it all wrong, but as he looked once more at all the dimly lit windows he knew that he couldn't take that chance. So many people were hidden away in these houses, old, young, little children, tiny babies, all at risk.

"Gotta get help!" he whispered to himself, and he turned and thundered back up the stairs to find Reuben.

"Listen to me," he said, his voice low and urgent. "There's going to be a landslip and it's starting now. You'll be safe here in this house, but the others won't. We've got to get all the people out of their houses, at once."

Reuben put down his plate and kipper bones and stared as though he thought him mad.

Sam bent down and pulled him to his feet. "Don't ask me how I know! I can't explain it, but please believe me – please." Then he spoke slowly and solemnly, trying to make it sound really serious. "Reuben, I bring you warning!"

Suddenly Reuben's mouth dropped open and at last he seemed to take notice. "Tha's not a devil, tha's … an angel?"

Sam almost wanted to laugh, he'd certainly never been called an angel before, but the situation was too urgent for laughter. "Yes," he said. "Yes, I am."

"I thought tha was clean," Reuben muttered. "If tha's really an angel, then I'll do anything tha tells me."

"We've got to get them out!" Sam cried. "How can we make them come out?"

"Shout fire!" said Reuben. "That'll fetch them out!"

They both tore down the street, banging on doors, shouting and bellowing.

"Fire! Fire and landslip! Get out! Get out!"

"Save theesens. Get out! Get out!"

Sam hadn't time to stop and think about it properly, but somewhere at the back of his mind he recognized the frantic rushing about in his dream. Now I know, he thought. Now I know what it was that I had to do.

They came slowly at first, but at last the sleepy people began to take notice. By the time the two boys had reached the sea end of the street, people were staggering out of their houses with candles and lanterns, wondering what was going on.

"Where's the fire?" they asked, but then they saw the crack in the road and watched as it grew wider.

An old fisherman shook his head and reminded them that houses on Henrietta Street *had* slipped into the sea once before, long ago.

People took notice of that and began flooding out of their houses. Mothers came running out with their babies; old people were wrapped in blankets and carried in their chairs. People in nightclothes, some half naked, came out into the freezing night, carrying their ornaments, their work tools and their furniture.

More shale started rolling down from the cliff and a crack appeared down the side of one of the houses. Sam hadn't been mistaken. He hadn't caused a panic for nothing. At last it seemed that everyone was out of their houses and heading fast for Church Street.

"Come back now!" Reuben shouted, turning back towards Church Street himself again. "Come back, Angel – the road is breaking up!"

Sam followed fast, but as he came close to the first crack that he'd seen, it suddenly widened and Sam found himself trapped and alone on the seaward side.

"Jump!" Reuben shouted. "Jump and I'll catch thee."

The ground rocked beneath his feet and the crack grew bigger. Sam fished in his pyjama pocket and pulled out his three precious pieces of jet. It was time for this angel to fly home and he'd better do it fast. He hurled the gleaming black lumps away from him, over the gaping earth, towards Reuben.

"Goodbye, jettie lad!" he shouted as he flung them, and all at once he went flying up into the air, and then back with a jolt into a warm dark place. He put out his hand and clicked on the small light inside the cubby-hole; his clothes were there, still hanging on their rail. He was quite relieved to see that the door at the back of the cupboard was locked again. He clambered shakily onto his bed and wearily crawled along – then slid in between the sheets, utterly exhausted, but with a growing sensation of warmth and satisfaction.

Chapter 11

Evidence

....

He woke quite late in the morning to another bright sunny day. Sam pulled himself up in bed, grinning stupidly. "Now *that*," he murmured, "*that* was a dream to beat them all."

He got out of bed and went straight to the cupboard, pulling the curtain back. He stared at the locked door for ages, then sighed. He was daft. Naomi had been right about that all along. He looked up at the carved angel's face above the doorway. "No wonder it looked familiar," he whispered.

At last he shook himself and reached towards the hangers for a clean T-shirt, but as he parted his clothes to get it out he saw something on the step in front of the door. Three gleaming black lumps lay neatly side by side, and as he crouched to examine them closely his heart thundered with joy.

Sam got dressed and went downstairs for some breakfast. He told his mother that he was going to see Naomi.

"Surprise, surprise," said Janet. "How are you going to manage without your dear Naomi when you get back to Sheffield?"

"I'll be coming here again," he told her. Nothing that Janet said could upset him this morning. He fished in his pocket and brought out one of his pieces of jet.

"For you," he said, putting it down in front of his sister.

Janet picked it up and her mouth dropped open wide.

"See you," Sam told her as he went out of the door.

He stood for a while staring down Henrietta Street, where the strong bank of boulders now kept the headland safe. He smiled, then turned and walked off towards Church Street. He called in on Mr Barker and asked if he wanted Snowy exercised today.

"It's good of you," Mr Barker said gloomily. "But I might as well take him for a walk myself. Nobody seems to want jet at the moment. They don't want to pay the price of good hand carving."

Sam looked around the cosy workshop, saddened by Mr Barker's despair. Then he remembered something that he'd heard when he was walking down Church Street just the day before. "I heard one of the goth girls saying how much she'd like to buy special goth jewellery made of Whitby jet."

"Ooh, they seem a strange lot to me, those goths," said Mr Barker. "But I've got to say that they do bring a bit of money into the town."

Sam thought hard about it. "Could you make necklaces of little black bats?" he asked.

Mr Barker looked surprised at the question. "Bats? I can make anything," he said.

"Well," said Sam. "That's the sort of thing they seem to like. I just think that necklaces of bats would sell really well to all these goths."

"Bats?" Mr Barker still sounded unimpressed.

"Yes, and perhaps there are other things. Ghosts, cats and little devils. You could make a special range of goth jewellery and call it Red Devil Jet!" said Sam.

Mr Barker smiled at that. "Red Devil? Now you're talking." He scratched his head, beginning to look interested, and Sam felt pleased to see the change in him.

"I'm sure they'd love it!" he insisted.

"Aye, lad, I think you've got something there. Bats, devils, cats … let me see… Owls? Ghostly castles?"

"Yes, that's right!" Sam could see that the old man was really catching on to his idea.

"The black dog?"

Sam looked puzzled.

"The famous Whitby black dog, that leapt

ashore from Dracula's ship when it ran
aground."

Then Sam remembered the Ghost Walk
man telling them all about it. "That's exactly
the right sort of thing," he agreed.

"Tell you what – you take Snowy out." Mr
Barker was grabbing pen and paper. "I'll have
a black dog designed when you come back."

Sam and Naomi wandered onto Tate Hill
Sands with Snowy sniffing at their heels. The
beach was full of goths all carrying plastic
bags; they were picking up rubbish.

"Good grief," said Naomi. "Now I've seen
it all."

They stared for a while, amazed at the
sight, then decided to walk along the pier.
They sat down on the seat at the end, where
Sam had first seen the two goths who had
startled him. Snowy lingered behind them,
sniffing at the crab pots.

Sam started trying to tell Naomi about
what had happened to him in the night, but it

was difficult. She went very quiet, looking out towards the lighthouses and the sea.

"It was a dream," she said, when at last he'd finished.

Sam sighed with disappointment. She wasn't laughing or being unkind, just sensible.

"Some dreams do feel very real," she added.

"I knew you'd think that," he whispered. "And I don't blame you."

"Well," Naomi said. "You know what Harry would say, don't you? Evidence! Where's your evidence?"

Sam shook his head and was silent for a moment or two, but then he put his hand into his pocket and pulled out one of the pieces of jet. "I *have* got something," he said. He held it out. "This is for you, anyway!"

Naomi gasped. The piece of jet had been delicately carved into a wreath of tiny corn stalks and in the middle was the name NAOMI.

"Got another bit," said Sam, and he

brought the last piece out from his pocket. This had an edging pattern full of movement. It looked like the waves of the sea and in the middle was carved the word ANGEL.

Naomi looked at Sam, doubtful at first, but then suddenly smiling. "Either you've turned into a fine jet carver overnight, or ... or perhaps what you've told me just might be true!"

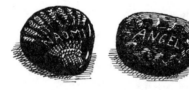

Author's Note

Though these characters and the jet workshop are all invented, a real Victorian Jet Works, similar to the one in my story, can be seen at the end of Church Street in Whitby. Beautiful examples of Victorian jet work can be seen in Whitby's Pannett Park Museum.

In 1870 many houses in Henrietta Street were destroyed in a landslip. Though a great deal of property was lost, warning was given, and no deaths were caused by the disaster.

The author would like to thank Hal Redvers-Jones and Alex MacKenzie of the Victorian Jet Works, 123B Church Street, Whitby.

The author would also like to thank Thomas M. V. Roe for sharing his knowledge of the jet industry and Whitby history.